Witch-in Training

Training

Brewing up

ROARING GOOD READS

Collins

🔲 *An imprint of HarperCollinsPublishers*

*Roaring Good Reads will fire the imagination of all young readers
– from short stories for children just starting to read on their own,
to first chapter books and short novels for confident readers.*
www.roaringgoodreads.co.uk

Also by Maeve Friel
Witch-in-Training: Flying Lessons
Witch-in-Training: Spelling Trouble
Witch-in-Training: Charming or What?

Other Roaring Good Reads from Collins

Mister Skip *by Michael Morpurgo*
Daisy May *by Jean Ure*
The Witch's Tears *by Jenny Nimmo*
Spider McDrew *by Alan Durant*
Dazzling Danny *by Jean Ure*

Witch-in-Training
Training
Brewing up

Maeve Friel

Illustrated by Nathan Reed

ROARING GOOD READS

Collins

🏰 *An imprint of HarperCollinsPublishers*

First published by Collins in 2003
Collins is an imprint of HarperCollins *Publishers* Ltd
77-85 Fulham Palace Road, Hammersmith, London W6 8JB

The HarperCollins website address is www.harpercollins.co.uk

1 3 5 7 9 8 6 4 2

Text copyright © Maeve Friel 2003
Illustrations by Nathan Reed 2003

ISBN 0 00 713344 8

The author asserts her moral right
to be identified as author of the work.

Printed and bound in England by
Clays Ltd, St Ives plc

Conditions of Sale
This book is sold subject to the condition
that it shall not, by way of trade or otherwise,
be lent, re-sold, hired out or otherwise circulated
without the publisher's prior consent in any form,
binding or cover other than that in which it is
published and without a similar condition
including this condition being imposed on the
subsequent purchaser.

Chapter One

Jessica lazily zigzagged over the roofs of the High Street, paused above Miss Strega's hardware shop and sniffed the air. "How odd," she thought as she zoomed down to the pavement and hopped off her broom.

"There's no smell of a bubbling cauldron. I thought I was to start my Brewing lessons today."

She sniffed once more – but there was nothing, not even a hint of Cold Smelly Voles – so she removed her flying helmet, helped Berkeley out of her pocket, lifted the door latch and hurried inside to find out what was going on.

To her surprise, Miss Strega was not in her usual place behind the shop counter. Instead, she was whizzing around, fast-forwarding,

reversing and zooming all over the place, pulling drawers open and scribbling notes on a clipboard. "Moonrays and marrowbones!" she was muttering. "What a mess!"

"What's a mess?" Jessica asked. "Have you lost something?"

Miss Strega swivelled around, peered over her glasses at Jessica, stuck her pencil behind her ear and swooped to the floor. "Three economy packets of owl feathers, two phials of Fairy Tears, half a Dragon's

Tooth, one Wasp Sting and eight Spider Egg Sacs. That's all!"

"That's all?" repeated Jessica, wondering what sort of spell Miss Strega was brewing up with that mixture.

Miss Strega waved a hand at the open drawers. "I'm talking about Brewing ingredients."

"Brewing ingredients?"

"By the hooting of Minerva's owl, Jess! You sound like an echo. Don't you understand this is an emergency! I've run out of everything from Mystic Biscuits to Teenage Slugs. We shall have to leave on a collecting trip at once."

"A collecting trip? Fantastic!" said Jessica who loved both travelling and shopping. "Where do we have to go?"

"The attic," said Miss Strega.

"The attic?" Jessica's face fell.

"You're still echoing me, dear. Now, on your marks." She tweaked the starter twigs on her broomstick. *"Ig-Fo-Li: Ignition, Forward* and *Lift."*

As Miss Strega rose majestically towards the ceiling, her cat Felicity, who had been snoozing on top of a pile of Spell books, launched herself on to the back of her broom. Jessica remounted her own broomstick and followed them as they disappeared through the trapdoor into the attic.

The attic smelt of old suitcases and dusty cauldrons – and cats, of course. Felicity was Miss Strega's number one shop cat, but there were always other cats in residence, cats on holiday or having kittens or in hiding. Jessica took one of them on her lap and sat down on a pile of moth-eaten cloaks while Miss Strega rummaged about behind a curtain of cobwebs.

"Here we are," she said at last. "This is what we want – the Expedition Kit." She began to haul out chests marked Samples and boxes marked Specimens, baskets of every shape and size, long-handled fishing nets and short-handled butterfly nets.

"And of course, we shall have to take the campfire cauldron." Miss Strega turned a small cooking pot upside down and whacked it.

Several cross spiders scuttled across the attic boards in search of cover. A family of bewildered sleepy mice, who had bedded down for the night, tumbled out on to the floor. Felicity and all the other cats immediately chased after them.

Once she had calmed everything down again, Miss Strega started loading her broomstick while Jessica inspected the Expedition Kit. Inside one of the boxes, she found rows and rows of glass jars and bottles, each labelled in Miss Strega's spidery handwriting, as well as tweezers and camel-hair brushes, pin cushions and tins of rubber bands.

"The plan," Miss Strega explained, "is to collect all the standard shop items..."

"Like Snails' Drool and Gnats' Spittle," suggested Jessica, reading the labels on the bottles.

"Exactly, but we'll scoot around looking for some new products as well..."

"...like the Conjuring Stones from Pelagia's beach or Dr Krank's Withershins Balls?"

Miss Strega nodded her long chin vigorously. "Absolutely! Witches World Wide like novelty as much as anyone. So, we'll need to fly off the usual flight paths and go to the Very End of the Earth."

"That sounds great," agreed Jessica as she hurriedly replaced the cork on a whiffy bottle labelled Aroma of Lion's Den. "But how on earth are we going to carry all this gear? Once these boxes and baskets are full, our broomsticks won't be able to lift off the ground."

"That's where the homing brooms come in." Miss Strega pointed at a pair of long-handled dusters leaning against the water tank and nodding their pink and grey feathered heads as they chatted. "They work rather like those racing pigeons that always know their way home," explained Miss Strega, ignoring Jessica's raised eyebrows. "Once we have collected enough stock, we send the brooms back with all our parcels; they'll come and go as often as we please."

Jessica whistled admiringly. The homing brooms turned a little pinker and bowed.

Miss Strega heaved the last of the boxes on to the back of her broom and handed

Jessica a large butterfly net. "You'll need that in a minute. Now, are we ready to fly? Are all your twig controls in working order? Have you got your flying helmet? Is your cloak clean?"

Jessica nodded, fastened the strap of her aerodynamic flying helmet under her chin and smoothed down the front of her silk Super-Duper De-Luxe Guaranteed-Invisibility -When-You-Need-It cape.

"Have you got your Spell book? Your wand? An owl feather in case you need to do some Mingling?"

Jessica nodded again, three times.

"Then, let's take to the sky. I think we might start our journey with a moon-vault."

Chapter Two

Jessica and Miss Strega perched on the tallest chimneypot and squinted at the sliver of banana-shaped moon. It was just visible behind a bank of damp black clouds.

"I think it's wobbling," Jessica said, doubtfully.

"Perhaps it isn't a good night for vaulting."

"Fiddlesticks. It's not wobbling; it's shimmering, just as I'd hoped. Nets aloft, please."

Miss Strega flew on to the peak of the roof tiles and shuffled along it, holding her butterfly net in one outstretched arm. Jessica shuffled along behind her, wondering what

on earth
(or on moon) the
nets were for.

When the planet Venus was lined up *precisely* at a right angle to the control twigs of their broomsticks, Miss Strega shouted, "Deploy your Moon-Vault twig, NOW."

Immediately, Jessica's plaits flew back over her shoulders and her scarf streamed out behind her back. It was like being on a rollercoaster with an invisible giant blowing into her face. Then she was off. She broke loose, shot up into the sky – and flew straight, bang, right into a cloud of sticky moondust.

"Hey!" she yelled at Miss Strega who was ducking and diving ahead of her, scooping up the dust in her net. "Hang on."

"No, you keep up," Miss Strega shouted back over her shoulder, "and catch as much of this dust as you can. I know it tickles but it's very popular with fairies. They think they look cute sprinkling it around wherever they go – so dust away, Jess."

There was nothing, absolutely nothing, cute about moondust, Jessica decided. It got everywhere, in her ears and her eyes and her socks and her hair and up her nose like summer midges in a Scottish bog. It wasn't tickly, but it was itchy, very itchy.

So Jess pulled her scarf up to her nose, closed her eyes and flailed about with her moondust net as best as she could.

When she opened her eyes again, she was already tumbling down the far side of the moon. The neon lights of an intergalactic highway lay ahead.

"The Milky Way!" she yelled, tossing her net of moondust to Miss Strega and zooming towards the Milky Way entrance.

As usual, there was a long tailback of fliers trying to get on to the Milky Way.

There were turbaned viziers on flying carpets, dreamy angels on fluffy clouds and a set of flying saucers. Jessica cruised to a pause behind a white winged horse that was pawing the ground impatiently.

Miss Strega came up behind her. "There," she said, flipping over the pages on her clipboard and putting a large tick beside Moondust. "One done, only 332 more to go. Now, what on earth is holding us up today?

Not another Phoenix rising, I hope."

"Look over there!" Jessica pointed towards the toll-bridge barrier where a large dragon with a very fat bottom had got stuck. Her scaly tail flicked nervously as she tried to reverse out, scattering scales everywhere.

Miss Strega tut-tutted. "Shame to see those going to waste, Jess. Perhaps you could zoom over and pick them up."

Jessica twiddled with her broom twigs,

took off at an unexpected angle – a sort of diagonal lift – twirled over the queue and swooped down behind the flustered dragon.

"Do you mind if I take some of your scales?" she asked, smiling her sweetest smile.

The dragon turned around, revealing a long mournful face and surprisingly bushy eyebrows. "You can have all the scales you want, Miss," she sniffed, "and if you can Spell me out of here, I'll tell you where you can get some Dragons' Teeth for nothing as well. I know you witches like a good supply of those."

"I'm only a witch-in-training," said Jessica, stuffing as many of the dragon's scales as she could into her saddlebag, "but I'll see what I can do." She took out her wand and waved it about. "This *should* work.

"With a wave of my wand, da-da.
A bang of my heels, bang-bang,
With a gnash of my teeth, clang-clang,
Three bats of my eyelids and a wink,
Your bottom will begin to shrink –
I think."

The dragon's bottom stopped thrashing around. Little by little, it began to shrink.

"Hey, steady on," said the dragon with a loud snort. "I don't want to be too bony. I've got to sleep on a lot of sharp metal objects. You don't want to be too thin if you live in a cold cave on top of a hoard of gold, you know."

"Right," said Jessica, with a giggle. "That should be enough."

With one final wriggle, the dragon was FREE. She flew off with her cheeks ablaze, snorting embarrassed plumes of smoke.

"Hang on," shouted Jessica, "what about the Dragons' Teeth?"

"Drop in to Torquemada, the dragon dentist," the dragon shouted back. "Tell him Gonzina sent you."

Chapter Three

Some time in the middle of the night, Jessica and Miss Strega flew over a walled city. Far below, Jessica could see high gabled houses with pointy eaves and a castle with turrets all lit up with double strings of yellow lanterns.

When Miss Strega gave the signal to descend, they landed on a chimney on a high rooftop and looked down at a huge cobbled square within the castle walls.

It was market day. Hundreds of stalls had been set up higgledy-piggledy in every bit of space. Jessica was amazed to see that every stallholder was wearing a tall conical hat, and that beside each stall, there stood a huge cauldron, hubbling and bubbling and giving off some very strange smells, not all of them delicious.

"It's a witches' market!" exclaimed Jessica.

"Not just any witches' market. It's the Market at the Very End of the Earth," said Miss Strega, with a contented sigh. "Let's go shopping!"

As soon as she hit the ground, Miss Strega behaved as if someone had switched her on to the spin cycle. She whizzed along the rows of stalls, elbows akimbo, stocking up on all sorts of leaves and shoots and barks and seeds. She hurtled across the bridges and up and down the castle battlements buying Mermaids' Gloves and Sphagnum Moss; Antler Tips and Reindeer Velvet; Poisonous Laurel and Deadly Nightshade. She sent a juggler flying and trampled on his collecting hat to reach the top of a queue for some very rare Scotch Bonnets. (These, she explained to Jessica, were vicious red peppers to tie the tongues of fibbers and spoofers.)

In no time at all, she had packages tucked under her arms, and bags hanging off her shoulders and her wrists, not to mention little parcels in every pocket of her cape. Jessica zoomed along behind her, loading up the homing brooms whenever Miss Strega looked as if she might collapse under the weight of all her purchases.

"I have a funny feeling," she thought as she watched Miss Strega open the drawstring of her purse for the umpteenth time, "that these market witches have put a Spell on us."

At that very moment, there was a loud violent explosion behind them. They swung around to see a saleswitch in front of a cauldron full of things popping and sneezing and leaping about.

"Snapping Hazelnuts from the witch-hazel tree!" the witch called out as she ladled the popping mix into paper pokes. "Don't go home without them. Only one maravedi the kilo."

Snapping
Hazelnuts
☆ ☆ ☆
1 Maravedi
the kilo!

"What are they for?" Jessica nudged Miss Strega.

Miss Strega looked a little sheepish. "Search me," she whispered. "I've never heard of them. See if it says anything in your Spell book."

Jessica took out her *Spelling Made Easy*. "'The Snapping Hazelnut or Hamamelis'," she read out, "'is the Universal Cure for swellings, burns, windy bottoms, scalds, night worries and sore eyes. Just add boiling water and the Snapping Hazelnut will do the rest.' Golly, it seems to fix just about everything."

"Absolutely," said the saleswitch, snatching a rogue hazelnut that snapped and crackled and spat out seeds as it tried to escape from its poke. "No witch's cupboard should be without them."

Miss Strega sighed and opened her purse once again. "I'd better take three kilos – but I won't pay more than two maravedis."

The next thing to catch their attention was a cauldron billowing clouds of steam and hot soapy bubbles. When they peered into it, they caught a glimpse of the heel of a striped sock, the toe of a football sock, the leg of a grey school sock, and then the lacy frill of a baby sock. They bobbed to the surface, one by one, then sank back beneath the bubbles once again.

"How curious!" Jessica declared.

"It's the Pool of Lost Socks," said the witch-in-charge, giving the cauldron a brisk stir with a wooden spoon. "All the odd socks in the world that ever go missing end up here."

"What do you use them for?" asked Jessica.

The witch winked. "Are there nights when ghostly footsteps drag up and down your staircase? When you can't sleep on account of screeching owls, howling wolves or singing cats?"

Jessica and Miss Strega nodded. "Singing cats especially," they said together. Felicity, curled up in the feathers of a homing broom, opened one orange eye and stuck her tongue out at them.

"Then what you need is one of these," said the witch. "A Putasockinit™, the enchanted sock, is guaranteed to reduce the volume of all nocturnal nuisances."

Jessica looked puzzled.

"It makes them shut up, I mean," explained the witch. "Just hang a Putasockinit™ on the end of your bed or put it in your muncheon and you can say goodbye to sleepless nights. Go on, take your pick." The Sock Witch tapped the lip of the cauldron and hundreds of socks bobbed up to the surface, all eager to be rescued and returned to a useful life, even without their twin.

Jessica fished one out. It was rather grey but had digital toes in the Witches World Wide colours of jade and purple, so it seemed a good choice. Miss Strega chose an emerald green one; she thought she might have owned it once so she was a bit miffed that she had to pay to have it back.

When Miss Strega was quite satisfied that she had inspected every market stall, she and Jessica headed for the shops under the arches. Tucked away in a dark corner, they came across a tiny shop that gave off the most wonderful smell. The witch-in-charge beckoned them in, scurried behind the counter and came back with a tray of little hard sugar cakes. But when Jessica made to take one, the witch grabbed her arm and gave her a wicked grin. "These are rompedenti, my dear. *You* don't want to eat them."

"Who are they for then?"

"Aaahh," said the witch, tapping her nose in the traditional way. "Just stamp the biscuit with the name of a person you want to cast a spell on, and within twelve hours, all their teeth will turn black and fall out. And the best thing is, there is no antidote."

"Great honking goose feathers!" said Jessica. "That's wicked."

"Spot on!" agreed Miss Strega. "They're bound to come in useful sometime. Three dozen, please."

Their next discovery was even more amazing. Down a blind alley, they stumbled across a stall of blankets.

"Going on a secret mission?" hissed the witch behind the stall. "Don't leave home without Cover of Darkness, the blanket that stretches to infinity and back again. Just wrap yourself and your broom in this and you'll be there and back before anyone knows you've left home."

"Every single one of my customers will want one of those!" Miss Strega declared delightedly. She whistled for the homing brooms to come and load up. "I'll have the lot."

Once Miss Strega had given the brooms their flight plans and waved them off, she turned to Jessica. "I don't know about you, my little lamb's lettuce," she said, "but my feet are killing me – let's have breakfast." And she steered Jessica towards the flickering neon lights of the Hags' Express Diner.

Chapter Four

The food in the Hags' Express Diner was
awful, and made even worse by an old
crone who sawed away tunelessly at a violin
all the time they were there. While Miss
Strega checked her shopping list on her

clipboard, Jessica riffled through the pages of her *Spelling Made Easy* and slyly dropped her untouched dumplings under the table for Felicity and Berkeley.

"What we need now are some of the old traditional Shock Brew ingredients," Miss Strega said, removing a bit of gristle from her teeth and reaching for her broom. "So we'd better take to the skies again."

"Hang on," said Jessica, pointing at a picture in her book. "What about the Dragons' Teeth that Gonzina told us about? It says here that if you plant Dragons' Teeth, they turn into heroes and builders-of-cities and bodyguards. There must be millions of witches who'd like one of those. Shouldn't we go and visit the dragon dentist, Torquemada?"

Miss Strega sighed. "Right," she said, slipping two rompedenti under her plate as a tip for the cook and the violin crone. "*Ig-Fo-Li* then. But be warned, dragons in their lairs can be very unpredictable."

Torquemada's dental clinic was in a cave deep in the middle of a dark secret forest. Jessica imagined that yellow-eyed wolves tiptoed in the shadows and sad wandering lost babes scattered breadcrumbs on the forest paths. It was so creepy that she put all her lucky charms on full alert, especially the lighthouse pin that Pelagia had given her and which was really a Safe Harbour Charm. If the dragon turned out to be cantankerous, all she had to do was blink and count to ten and she could fly away to safety.

But Torquemada's lair was not as terrifying as she had feared. When Jessica and Miss Strega flew in, there was just one

old toothless dragon sitting on a hoard of gold. He looked up from the newspaper he was reading, evidently not a bit surprised by the unexpected arrival of two witches, and pointed at the headline:

DRAGON AUTHORITY DENIES
EXISTENCE OF ST GEORGE.

"What do they know?" he lisped. "It was that St George that smote me with his sword. Broke my jaw and all my teeth. My life as a dentist has been ruined. Ruined."

Jessica and Miss Strega looked at one another. The dragon with no teeth was Torquemada. The dragon dentist. As it turned out, having no teeth was only one of Torquemada's problems.

"I haven't always been a dentist, you know," he wheezed when they explained why they had come. "I was a warrior once. But a lifetime of breathing fire has done me in. I've permanent heartburn, my breath is nasty, my nostril hairs are all singed, my throat aches, I've terrible wind, and, I'm sorry, I *know* my cave smells like old fireworks."

Torquemada, Jessica and Miss Strega all gloomily gazed at the blackened walls, the soot dust that lay everywhere, the scorched furniture.

"And, as you can see, business is awful so I can't *give* you any samples," he lisped gummily. "But I'm happy to *trade* some dragon products if you can Brew up something to Spell some of my troubles away."

Miss Strega stroked her chin thoughtfully. She really was very keen to get some Dragons' Teeth now that she had come this far. "Hamamelis!  Snapping Hazelnuts!" she shouted. "The Universal Cure! Fetch me a cauldron at once and I'll Brew up. That ought to fix everything.

Except your teeth. I fear they are as lost and gone as the snowmen of yesteryear."

Before you could say "Winking cats and frisky bats", Miss Strega and Jessica had a pot of Snapping Hazelnut Syrup brewing up. As Jessica Mingled the explosive mixture, Miss Strega chanted,

"Burns, scalds, windy bottom or very sore eyes,
At the snap of these Hazelnuts
De-ma-te-ri-a-lize!"

She made Torquemada take three large tablespoonfuls at once, carefully poured the rest into a brown bottle and wrote out the instructions on the label.

The dragon was so grateful that he got out a box containing baby Dragons' Teeth and some interesting adult dragon extractions. "Take your pick," he urged Miss Strega through little puffs of smoke, "and, because I like you," he went on, "I'll give you some Dragon's Blood as well."

"What can we do with that?" asked Jessica, doubtfully, as she watched him decanting some green sticky goo from a big barrel into a tray of little bottles.

"Two things," he replied with a polite burp. "First, you can add a few drops to your bath water to protect yourself from injury – but be sure to immerse yourself completely. One unfortunate princess forgot to wash her ears."

"And what happened to her?" enquired Miss Strega.

"Let's just say, after the Bad Fairy put the Wart Maker Spell on her, she didn't look too pretty. Princess Cauliflower, they call her now."

Miss Strega shuddered. "And the second thing?"

"Well, a strong solution of Dragon's Blood can be used to make things invisible, especially print. So it's excellent for sending private messages, secret instructions, treasure maps." As he spoke, he rubbed a bit of the goo over the instructions on the medicine bottle and, as he had said, the writing disappeared.

"Golly, that's nifty," Miss Strega whistled and tucked the bottles of Dragon's Blood into her saddlebag. "Now, we'd love to stay and chat, Torquemada, but we must fly. Do keep taking that Snapping Hazelnut mixture."

Jessica and Miss Strega mounted their broomsticks and carefully edged their way towards the cave exit, taking care not to touch the sooty walls. At the door, Jessica turned back. "By the way, what do you use to *restore* the writing?"

Torquemada looked glum. "Mandragora. The Mandrake Root."

Miss Strega gasped.

Mandrake Root was the most valuable magic ingredient in the whole W3 Rule Book – and the most difficult to find. If she could find some Mandrake Root, she'd be the richest witch in the Witches World Wide Web. "You don't say! You know where the mandrake grows?"

"Sadly, no," Torquemada looked glummer than ever. "You see, the mandrake stinks to high heaven and since I can't smell anything any more, it's years since I've been able to find any. But the forest used to be full of it. By the way, what did it say on this medicine bottle?"

But Miss Strega and Jessica had already fast-forwarded out of the door.

All that night, they blundered about on their brooms in the mist searching for the mandrake until, just before dawn, they spotted a red glow down by the swampy shores of a dark lake.

"It might be the mandrake, or it might not, but it's worth having a look. *Re-Pa-De*, please," Miss Strega declared, giving the order to *Reverse, Pause* and *Descend*.

They smelt the mandrake  long before they saw its red glow again – as Torquemada had warned, its leaves gave off an awful pong. Felicity clapped both her paws over her nose and Berkeley

flew off squawking in disgust.

But worse was to come. As soon as Miss Strega and Jessica tried to pull it out of the ground, the plant began to shriek. It shrieked and roared and screamed, "Blue murder!"

Behind them, in the swamp, Jessica and Miss Strega could hear rustlings, scamperings, all manner of footsteps, and twigs snapping. They looked around nervously as a hundred eyes bored into their backs.

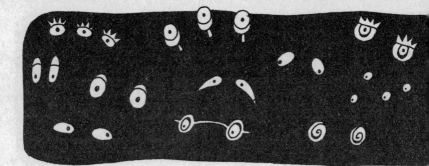

"Moonbones and marrowrays," whispered Miss Strega, all in a flutter. "What shall we do? There are hundreds of *whatevers* out there watching us. We should never have sent the Cover of Darkness blankets back with the homing brooms. In fact, I haven't got a single thing to Spell or Brew us out of this mess."

"Don't worry," Jessica whispered back. "I've got my Safe Harbour Charm and I'll activate it right now. Felicity, get back on the broom. Berkeley, pocket! Miss Strega, hold my hand."

Jessica blinked and counted to ten backwards. When she opened her eyes, the forest had quite disappeared and they were flying over a pretty valley of orange orchards.

Miss Strega paused her broom and fanned herself with her hat. "Ooof! All that shopping and excitement has worn me out. I could do with a good Brew," she said. "Let's pitch camp down there beside the river. We'll make some muncheon and have a Brewing Workshop."

"Brilliant," said Jessica, putting her broom into fast-descend.

Chapter Five

Jessica had not always loved camping. Before she met Miss Strega, she hated it. The tent was always falling down. The ground sheet leaked. The fire wouldn't light properly and the smoke got in everyone's eyes. But now that she was a witch-in-training, she knew that Charming was the name of the game. With the help of the tips she had picked up from Pelagia at Charm School, she soon had the tent pitched, the hammocks strung up, the mosquito nets in place and a jug of freshly squeezed orange juice cooling in a pool in the river.

Meanwhile, with a wave of her wand and a Spell or two, Miss Strega got a cauldron of muncheon bubbling on the campfire. (Muncheon, if you don't know, is what witches eat at night-time under the moon and the stars and is Jessica's favourite meal of the day.) The marvellous thing about muncheon is that it tastes of whatever you want. So from the same pot, Miss Strega could enjoy a soufflé with smelly blue cheese while Jessica could have spaghetti and meatballs, with double chocolate chip ice cream to follow.

Then Miss Strega set up a little light show of falling stars just for fun and turned the moonlight to 'mellow'. Berkeley was so enchanted she perched on the top of a mandarin tree and sang a selection of her own compositions in her very best silvery voice. (The bad news was that Felicity joined in too until Jessica threw an orange at her and got the Putasockinit™ out of her saddlebag. Felicity promptly decided to leg it and hunt lizards instead.)

Finally Miss Strega set up the Brewing Workshop around the campfire. Jessica waited patiently on a three-legged stool with her arms wrapped around her knees, all excited. Like any witch-in-training, she was dying to make a Brew full of nasty things like Eye of Newt, Rat Droppings and Goblin Snot, even if it was a bit pongy and disgusting.

"Now, let's begin," Miss Strega began, tapping the rim of her Brewing cauldron with her long owl feather.

"Are we going to make a Shock Brew?" asked Jessica, excitedly.

Miss Strega sniffed loudly. "No, we are not. Back in the old days, when witches still flew their broomsticks the wrong-way-round, the Shock Brew was all there was. In its day, it was very useful. However, I like to think we're all Modern Witches now."

Jessica looked a bit disappointed but she nodded loyally. Although Miss Strega was very, very old – she had been running her hardware shop since 991 – she didn't like anyone to think she was *at all* old-fashioned.

Miss Strega continued, tapping her nose wisely, "In fact, I've been giving the matter a lot of thought and I've invented the Modern Witch's Brewing Pyramid." She flipped over a page on her easel, drew a large pyramid and divided it into seven wide bands which she labelled Animal, Vegetable, Mineral, Smell, Noise, Liquid and Seasoning. "There are the seven essential things every Brewing Spell must include, whether it is a good Spell, a wicked Spell or a mischievous Spell."

Jessica nodded again although she really hadn't a clue what Miss Strega was talking about.

Miss Strega continued. "Starting at the narrow top end, you choose a little *animal* extract or tissue, just a *small* tube of Snails' Drool, say..."

ANIMAL: a SMALL tube of Snails' Drool

and then, as you move down the pyramid, you can use more and more of each category, for example, a *cup* of Buttercup Dew for your *vegetable* bit..."

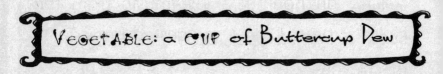

VEGETABLE: a CUP of Buttercup Dew

"...then maybe a *handful* of Moondust for your mineral."

MINERAL: a HANDFUL or two of Moondust

"For the fourth band, you can use as much smell as you like, say the *whole bottle* of that Aroma of Lion's Den you sniffed in the attic."

"Or the pong of Torquemada's cave? Or the stink of the mandrake leaves?" quipped Jess.

"Exactly so." Miss Strega filled in the smell band.

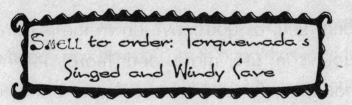

SMELL to order: Torquemada's
Singed and Windy Cave

"Next comes as much noise as you want."

"Like an hour of fiddle music from the Hags' Express Diner?" suggested Jessica.

"Bravo Jess! You're getting the hang of this."

Noise as desired: the Hags' Express
Diner's Terrible Fiddler

"Then pour in plenty of water or whatever."

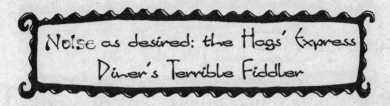

PLENTY OF WATER: seawater,
ditchwater, well water, ill water

"Hot or cold?" asked Jess.

Miss Strega stroked her long chin. "Why don't you find yourself a cauldron and make up a

Brew yourself to see how it works." She filled in the seventh band of the pyramid and ripped off the page. "Use whatever you can find in the orchard. And remember, a good brewer always adds that special *something*, a bit of herself."

"Mmm," thought Jessica, taking the page from Miss Strega and reading the bottom line.

SEASON thoroughly with a Spell and Mingle well.

She knitted her brows. "What kind of seasoning? What sort of Spell would you like me to make?"

But Miss Strega had already picked up her book (*The Brewing Year* by Delia Catessen) and wasn't listening.

Jessica picked up a cauldron and set off to make her Pyramid Brew. She hadn't gone very far before she found a very interesting snakeskin. It was quite transparent and had bulges where the snake's eyes would have been before it had slithered off in its shiny new skin. Perfect for the Animal bit. Then she gathered a handful of scarlet poppy flowers and scooped up a trowel of red earth. That took care of the Vegetable and Mineral bits. Next in were the smells of the orchard – a good whiff: clementine blossom and burning orange wood. For noise, she added all the sounds of the orchard, the whoosh of a cloud of crickets rising, a far-off donkey

braying and eight tolls from the village bell. After that, she filled the cauldron to the brim with lots of clear water from the river.

"This is too nice," she thought, frowning. "Not a bit like a Shock Brew." She read the last line of the Brewing Pyramid diagram again.

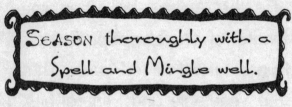

SEASON thoroughly with a Spell and Mingle well.

She glanced over at Miss Strega, quietly reading beside the campfire; at Berkeley trilling on the clementine tree; at Felicity watching her own reflection in the river and at the homing brooms just coming in to land. It was all far too charming.

"Have you finished yet?" Miss Strega called out over her reading glasses. "Muncheon's ready."

Jessica picked up her long-eared owl Mingling feather. "What this needs," she thought, "is a bit of me. Some seasoning to give it a bit of oomph, something like the Wart Maker Spell, or the Lifelong Hat Hair Curse.

Or maybe a non-stop Sneeze Attack. Because I am a *witch* after all, not a good fairy with a sticky-out dress and silly moondust."

She pondered for a moment more, and then intoned:

"Biting lice, sucking lice,
true bugs and beetles,
Grasshoppers, stick insects,
mantis and locusts,
Fleas and mosquitoes,
thistles and burrs,
Hairy pullovers and spindly
dwarf furze."

Her fingers moved rapidly over the cauldron as she Mingled her Spell. If anyone had been watching her, they would have seen that she was smiling a very old-fashioned witchy smile.

The spell began to work in the middle of the night.

First the homing brooms began to shudder and shake their feathery heads.

Then, out of the blue, Felicity leapt out of her hammock and dashed off. Jessica could hear her frantically rubbing her back against the trunk of a nearby tree.

Berkeley was restless too, fidgeting and moving about in Jessica's pocket. Suddenly, she shot out and began to groom and poke at her feathers. "Hu-eet," she complained, trying to dislodge imaginary balls of pocket fluff and bird seed from under her wings. Eventually, she flew off to sing protest songs from a perch on a telegraph wire.

Miss Strega was not happy either. She tossed and turned and scratched between her shoulder blades with a long bony finger.

"Pesky mosquitoes," she muttered, jabbing at her back with the point of her wand.

Jessica smiled to herself in the warm silent darkness. "No, not mosquitoes. It's the Modern Witch's Pyramid Brew with added twenty-four hour Out-of-Reach Itch!"

Chapter Six

In the morning, Jessica woke to find Miss Strega writing out a list of things for Jessica to find in the orchard.

"These," Miss Strega said, poking at an itch behind her knee, "are the kind of things the common or garden witch likes to keep in her stock cupboard. Even we Modern Witches need them too in small doses."

Jessica read the list and wrinkled her nose. "Beetles, Crickets, Moth Wings, Spider Silk, Gnats' Spittle... I'm not killing anything," she said sharply.

"Did I ask you to?" Miss Strega peered over the top of her spectacles. "Seek and you will find."

Jessica soon discovered an interesting thing about hunting and collecting. Wherever she went, crawling under the orange trees or peering into the ditches, she found what she was looking for. There were shiny beetles with bodies of metallic green armour, crickets which looked like dried papery leaves, moths with delicate transparent wings and huge webs of spider silk dangling between trees with their dead owners shrivelled up like dried raisins. Her specimen boxes were half full before Berkeley had even returned from her night out.

Miss Strega busied herself bottling dew and gathering seedpods from the magic jacaranda trees. Needless to say, it was Jessica who had to collect all the disgusting things like snails' drool, *and* persuade every gnat in the orchard to spit into a glass bottle. When a herd

of bearded goats strolled past, swishing their tails, it was Jessica again who had to follow them and pick up their droppings with tweezers. Miss Strega just whistled old Brewing songs, filled matchboxes with nice clean poppy seeds and scratched and poked and prodded between her shoulder blades.

"Perhaps, the Modern Witch's Pyramid Brew is a good idea, after all," Jessica huffed.

"Actually, some day you may find the goats' poo very useful," Miss Strega declared. "Say a gang of rude goblins is partying on your rooftop, or the coven at the crossroads are screaming like banshees, a goats' poo stink potion will soon send them packing."

At last, when the homing brooms were loaded – and it was not that easy because they were both so itchy that they complained and squirmed and shook their feathery heads like wet dogs trying to get water out of their ears – Miss Strega consulted her clipboard once again.

"What a marvabulous expedition this is turning out to be. I now have Toenail of Wild Boar, (that's very rare, it's sure to fetch a good price), a selection of Hedgehog Spikes, a bunch of Tail Feathers from a White Crow, an excellent assortment of Calls by an Owl perched on an ivy-covered tower at Dead of Night, (and you can't get eerier than that), a Fright of Bats on the Wing, Gnats' Spittle and..."

She stopped ticking things off her list and poked the middle of her back with the end of a butterfly net. "By Walpurga's blessed warts, I won't be sorry to leave this place. I've been itchy all day. Could you scratch my back for me, Jess? Down a bit, that's better, no it isn't, up a bit, no, down, just a little to the left..."

"Have you decided where we are going next?" Jessica asked mid-scratch.

Miss Strega didn't answer at once. She had

just caught sight of Felicity who was behaving very strangely, alternately rubbing behind her ears and break-dancing along the paths between the trees. Slowly she turned around to face Jessica – and was surprised to see that Berkeley was upside down in her pocket, flinging things over her shoulders. First, Jessica's Nutmeg Charm flew out, then a cloud of fluff balls, an explosion of birdseed and, last of all, a round pebble with a tiny hole in it.

Jessica turned a little red as she bent down to pick up her lucky pebble and her anti-hair-tangle Nutmeg Charm. "I'm so sorry – Berkeley seems to be spring-cleaning her pocket. She says her bed is scratchy."

Miss Strega pursed her lips and looked quizzically at Jessica. "But you haven't been feeling itchy? No? Fancy that

when all the rest of us, even the homing brooms, are under attack by invisible pests."

When Jessica said nothing, Miss Strega

tapped the two homing brooms with her wand to send them on their way, and mounted her own broomstick. "By the way, what spell did you put in that brew you gave us all last night?"

"I just made a mixture. I didn't have time to add the Spell before muncheon." Jessica fibbed.

"Right." Miss Strega jabbed at the middle of her back again with her wand. Her voice was quite frosty. "It's time to go. I've some pressing business back at the shop."

"Oops," thought Jessica. She had a sudden flashback to an unfortunate accident she once had with a transformation spell, when she turned Miss Strega into a wasp! "I think she knows I've been up to something."

Chapter Seven

Back in her High Street shop, Miss Strega soon cheered up. The twenty-four hour Out-of-Reach Itch had worn off, so that helped. She sang jolly songs as she sorted and stored away all her new stock. She hummed, la-de-da, while she Brewed and bottled Snapping Hazelnut Syrup, the Universal Cure. She made little giggly noises as she stirred a cauldron in which she was making up a Brew with a recipe from *The Brewing Year* by Delia Catessen. Her Mingling feather flew backwards and forwards, round and round, crissed and crossed and did figures-of-eight.

"There's nothing like some home Brew when you return from a long trip," she chirruped contentedly although she didn't tell Jessica *what* she was brewing up. Strange spicy aromas wafted around the shop.

Jessica was pleased to be back too. She sat cross-legged on the counter, with Felicity purring on her lap and Berkeley snoozing in her pocket. She sowed a few of the Dragons' Teeth in small flower pots and put a notice in the window.

Dragons' Teeth - Grow your own hero.

Then she made labels for the bottles of Dragon's Blood.

Miss Strega's Brew hubbled and bubbled, toiled and boiled. "Is it a bit too gloopy?" she muttered to herself from time to time. "Or possibly not gloopy enough? It won't do if it's lumpy but, on the other hand, it's no good if it's runny."

At last, with one final loop-the-loop, Miss Strega pronounced the Brew ready. "I'm sure it will be perfectly galloobious," she said, pouring some of the Brew into a small cup and passing it to Jessica. "Down the hatch."

Jessica took the cup.

"Hu-eet," whistled Berkeley, soaring up to perch on a hook on the ceiling.

Felicity stretched, yawned, gave an orange wink and jumped on to the ground. The homing brooms stopped chatting.

Miss Strega's eyes seemed awfully twinkly. The shop was so quiet you could have heard a snail squeal.

Jessica sniffed the brew. "It smells delicious," she said but really she was thinking, "Something is not right, Miss Strega is up to something."

"Go on then. Knock it back."

The Brew almost took Jessica's head off. It first hit her on that wobbly thing at the back of her throat. "Aaaaagh," she went but no sound came out. It spread from the very tip of her tongue to the insides of her cheeks, along her gums and down her oesophagus.

Her eyes watered. She was sure smoke must be pouring out of her ears. Her tongue rolled up and tied itself into a hot knot. She leapt off the counter. "Water," she screamed but no sound came out.

Miss Strega tapped the side of her nose. "Never bewitch a witch," she said. "They tend to Spell back."

"Aaagh," screamed Jessica silently. Her whole head was on fire. At that very moment, she remembered the Scotch Bonnets from the Market at the Very End of the Earth.

She snatched a piece of paper from the counter and wrote urgently:

"I am very sorry for telling a fib. I put a twenty-four hour itch spell on all of you. Please, please, please forgive me."

She underlined the pleases three times.

Fireworks were exploding in her mouth. Her tongue flared red. Her gums smouldered.

"Hu-eet," Berkeley pleaded, fluttering around Miss Strega's head. The homing brooms cooed and shivered their feathery heads. Even Felicity looked worried.

Miss Strega gave them all a meaningful stare.

"Hu-eeeet," begged Berkeley.

"Fine," said Miss Strega, reaching for a bottle of Hamamelis and filling Jessica's cup. "You seem to be forgiven. Have some Snapping Hazelnut Syrup and take a break. I'm going up to the attic to put away the Expedition Kit." And she sailed up to the attic trapdoor followed by the homing brooms carrying all the baskets and boxes and nets.

Jessica clambered back on to the counter again. She was feeling a bit huffy and a bit weepy, a bit sorry and a bit cross. She looked at *The Brewing Year* which Miss

Strega had left lying open at the recipe for *The Scotch Bonnet Brew for tying the tongues of fibbers and spoofers*. She looked at the bottles of Dragon's Blood.

"Never bewitch a witch. They spell back," she remarked to nobody in particular. Then, very deliberately, she picked up one of the bottles, uncorked it and sprinkled several drops all over the page. She was very pleased to see the writing grow fuzzy, fade and disappear.

"That's got rid of that," she said to Felicity and Berkeley, "and what's more, we don't have any Mandrake Root to restore it."

Miss Strega came back at that very moment. She was carrying a tray in both hands and had a rolled-up piece of parchment tucked under one arm. "Now, my little sugar plum, before you go home, I have something for you," she said, setting the tray down on the counter and waving the piece of parchment at Jessica. "It's a certificate for completing your first training course. I'll just sign it and then we can have a little celebration."

THE STREGA WITCH-TRAINING ACADEMY
CERTIFICATE OF ATTENDANCE
THIS IS TO CERTIFY THAT
MISS JESSICA DIAMOND
HAS SUCCESSFULLY COMPLETED TRAINING IN
FLYING, SPELLING, CHARMING AND BREWING
STAGE 1
GRADE: GOLD STAR

SIGNED..

Miss Strega carefully unrolled the certificate, put a bell on one corner to hold it flat and took her pen out from behind her ear. As she did so, she noticed the uncorked bottle of Dragon's Blood and the blank page of *The Brewing Year*, where Jessica had deleted the Scotch Bonnet Brew. "Mmmm," she said, and stroked her long chin thoughtfully.

Jessica started inspecting Felicity's ears.

After a long pause, Miss Strega dipped her pen in the ink bottle and signed her name in her usual spidery writing. *Bella Strega*

"Congratulations, Jess," she said.

Jessica turned a little pink and curtsied.

"And now, let's have that celebration." Miss Strega poured out two thimblefuls of Cold Smelly Voles and offered Jessica a plate of biscuits. "Have a biscuit," she said. "There are

orange jambarollies and some new ones I've iced myself."

Jessica's fingers hovered over the plate of biscuits. They all looked yummy, especially the iced ones that had her name carefully picked out in Miss Strega's writing. She narrowed her eyes to have a better look – then chose an orange jambarollie.

"You wouldn't really have let me eat a rompedenti?" she said in a shocked voice. "My teeth could have turned black and fallen out!"

Miss Strega stroked her chin again, as if giving the matter her serious consideration. Then she raised her cup of Cold Smelly Voles. "Just testing," she said, grinning, "to keep you on your toes. Cheers!"

"Cheers," replied Jessica, grinning back. But just to be on the safe side, she poured the rest of the Dragon's Blood over the plate of biscuits. "Never bewitch a witch," she said, "or even a witch-in-training!"

Witch-in-Training
Flying Lessons

Maeve Friel

Illustrated by Nathan Reed

On Jessica's tenth birthday she discovers that she is a witch! With Miss Strega as her teacher, and a broomstick to fly, Jessica is ready to begin her training. The first book in a magical new series.

ISBN 0 00 713341 3

📚 *An imprint of* HarperCollins*Publishers*

www.roaringgoodreads.co.uk

Witch-in-Training
Spelling Trouble

Maeve Friel

Illustrated by Nathan Reed

Jesssica's Spelling Lesson is going horribly wrong.
Miss Strega is trying to teach her Transformation
Spells, using the Wand Method, but she's in such a
grump that Jessica can't seem to do anything right.
The second book about this lively young witch.

ISBN 0 00 713342 1

An imprint of HarperCollinsPublishers

www.roaringgoodreads.co.uk

Witch-in-Training
Charming or What?

Maeve Friel

Illustrated by Nathan Reed

Jesssica is at summer school with an exciting new teacher, Pelagia, who used to be a pirate! Jess thinks lessons on Incantations, Talismans, Oracles and Fortune Telling are much more exciting than Maths and History, and she soon puts her new skills to use. Jess's third adventure as she learns to be a witch.

ISBN 0 00 713343-X

ROARING GOOD READS

Collins

An imprint of HarperCollinsPublishers

www.roaringgoodreads.co.uk

Order Form

To order direct from the publishers, just make a list of the titles you want and fill in the form below:

Name ....

Address ....

....

....

Send to: Dept 6, HarperCollins Publishers Ltd, Westerhill Road, Bishopbriggs, Glasgow G64 2QT.

Please enclose a cheque or postal order to the value of the cover price, plus:

UK & BFPO: Add £1.00 for the first book, and 25p per copy for each additional book ordered.

Overseas and Eire: Add £2.95 service charge. Books will be sent by surface mail but quotes for airmail despatch will be given on request.

A 24-hour telephone ordering service is available to holders of Visa, MasterCard, Amex or Switch cards on 0141- 772 2281.

An imprint of HarperCollins Publishers